THE PETER RABBIT
COLORING BOOK

by Beatrix Potter ✳ Illustrated by Charles Santore

APPLESAUCE PRESS

Kennebunkport, Maine

The Tale of Peter Rabbit

ONCE UPON A TIME there were four little Rabbits, and their names were—Flopsy, Mopsy, Cotton-tail, and Peter.

They lived with their Mother in a sand-bank, underneath the root of a very big fir-tree.

"Now, my dears," said old Mrs. Rabbit one morning, "you may go into the fields or down the lane, but don't go into Mr. McGregor's garden: your Father had an accident there; he was put in a pie by Mrs. McGregor."

"Now run along, and don't get into mischief. I am going out."

Then old Mrs. Rabbit took a basket and her umbrella, and went through the wood to the baker's. She bought a loaf of brown bread and five currant buns.

Flopsy, Mopsy, and Cotton-tail, who were good little bunnies, went down the lane to gather blackberries:

But Peter, who was very naughty, ran straight away to Mr. McGregor's garden, and squeezed under the gate!

First he ate some lettuces and some French beans; and then he ate some radishes;

And then, feeling rather sick, he went to look for some parsley.

But round the end of a cucumber frame, whom should he meet but Mr. McGregor!

Mr. McGregor was on his hands and knees planting out young cabbages, but he jumped up and ran after Peter, waving a rake and calling out, "Stop thief!"

Peter was most dreadfully frightened; he rushed all over the garden, for he had forgotten the way back to the gate.

He lost one of his shoes among the cabbages, and the other shoe amongst the potatoes.

After losing them, he ran on four legs and went faster, so that I think he might have got away altogether if he had not unfortunately run into a gooseberry net, and got caught by the large buttons on his jacket. It was a blue jacket with brass buttons, quite new.

Peter gave himself up for lost, and shed big tears; but his sobs were overheard by some friendly sparrows, who flew to him in great excitement, and implored him to exert himself.

Mr. McGregor came up with a sieve, which he intended to pop upon the top of Peter; but Peter wriggled out just in time, leaving his jacket behind him.

And rushed into the tool-shed, and jumped into a can. It would have been a beautiful thing to hide in, if it had not had so much water in it.

Mr. McGregor was quite sure that Peter was somewhere in the tool-shed, perhaps hidden underneath a flower-pot. He began to turn them over carefully, looking under each.

Presently Peter sneezed—"Kertyschoo!" Mr. McGregor was after him in no time.

And tried to put his foot upon Peter, who jumped out of a window, upsetting three plants. The window was too small for Mr. McGregor, and he was tired of running after Peter. He went back to his work.

Peter sat down to rest; he was out of breath and trembling with fright, and he had not the least idea which way to go. Also he was very damp with sitting in that can.

After a time he began to wander about, going lippity—lippity—not very fast, and looking all around.

He found a door in a wall; but it was locked, and there was no room for a fat little rabbit to squeeze underneath.

An old mouse was running in and out over the stone doorstep, carrying peas and beans to her family in the wood. Peter asked her the way to the gate, but she had such a large pea in her mouth that she could not answer. She only shook her head at him. Peter began to cry.

Then he tried to find his way straight across the garden, but he became more and more puzzled. Presently, he came to a pond where Mr. McGregor filled his water-cans. A white cat was staring at some goldfish, she sat very, very still, but now and then the tip of her tail twitched as if it were alive. Peter thought it best to go away without speaking to her; he had heard about cats from his cousin, little Benjamin Bunny.

He went back towards the tool-shed, but suddenly, quite close to him, he heard the noise of a hoe— scr-r-ritch, scratch, scratch, scritch. Peter scuttered

underneath the bushes. But presently, as nothing happened, he came out, and climbed upon a wheelbarrow and peeped over. The first thing he saw was Mr. McGregor hoeing onions. His back was turned towards Peter, and beyond him was the gate!

Peter got down very quietly off the wheelbarrow; and started running as fast as he could go, along a straight walk behind some black-currant bushes.

Mr. McGregor caught sight of him at the corner, but Peter did not care. He slipped underneath the gate, and was safe at last in the wood outside the garden.

Mr. McGregor hung up the little jacket and the shoes for a scare-crow to frighten the blackbirds.

Peter never stopped running or looked behind him till he got home to the big fir-tree.

He was so tired that he flopped down upon the nice soft sand on the floor of the rabbit-hole and shut his eyes. His mother was busy cooking; she wondered what he had done with his clothes. It was the second little jacket and pair of shoes that Peter had lost in a fortnight!

I am sorry to say that Peter was not very well during the evening.

His mother put him to bed, and made some camomile tea; and she gave a dose of it to Peter!

"One table-spoonful to be taken at bed-time."

But Flopsy, Mopsy and Cotton-tail had bread and milk and blackberries for supper.

ONCE UPON A TIME there were four little Rabbits, and their names were—Flopsy, Mopsy, Cotton-tail, and Peter.

They lived with their Mother in a sand-bank, underneath the root of a very big fir-tree.

Flopsy, Mopsy, and Cotton-tail, who were good little bunnies, went down the lane to gather blackberries:

But Peter, who was very naughty, ran straight away to Mr. McGregor's garden, and squeezed under the gate!

First he ate some lettuces and some French beans; and then he ate some radishes;

But round the end of a cucumber frame, whom should he meet but Mr. McGregor!

Mr. McGregor was on his hands and knees planting out young cabbages, but he jumped up and ran after Peter, waving a rake and calling out, "Stop thief!"

Peter was most dreadfully frightened; he rushed all over the garden, for he had forgotten the way back to the gate.

I think he might have got away altogether if he had not unfortunately run into a gooseberry net. Peter shed big tears; but his sobs were overheard by some friendly sparrows, who implored him to exert himself.

Peter wriggled out just in time, leaving his jacket behind him, and rushed into the tool-shed, and jumped into a can.

Mr. McGregor was after him in no time and tried to put his foot upon Peter, who jumped out of a window.

The window was too small for Mr. McGregor, and he was tired of running after Peter. He went back to his work.

After a time he began to wander about, he found a door in a wall; but it was locked. An old mouse was running over the stone doorstep; Peter asked her the way to the gate, but she only shook her head at him. Peter began to cry.

Then he tried to find his way straight across the garden, and presently, he came to a pond where Mr. McGregor filled his water-cans. A white cat was staring at some goldfish. Peter thought it best to go away without speaking to her.

He went back towards the tool-shed, but suddenly, quite close to him, he heard the noise of a hoe and saw Mr. McGregor hoeing onions. Peter started running as fast as he could go. He slipped underneath the gate, and was safe at last in the wood outside the garden.

Peter never stopped running or looked behind him till he got home to the big fir-tree.

His mother put him to bed, and made some camomile tea for Peter! But Flopsy, Mopsy, and Cotton-tail had bread and milk and blackberries for supper.

BEATRIX POTTER (1866-1943) was a British author and illustrator who is best known for writing children's books featuring the adventures of animals such as Peter Rabbit, Benjamin Bunny, and Jeremy Fisher.

CHARLES SANTORE is a renowned children's book illustrator whose work has been widely exhibited in museums and celebrated with recognitions such as the prestigious Hamilton King Award, the Society of Illustrators Award of Excellence, and the Original Art 2000 Gold Medal from the Society of Illustrators. Santore illustrated the *New York Times* #1 bestselling edition of *The Night Before Christmas*, and is best known for his luminous interpretations of classic children's stories such as *The Classic Tale of Peter Rabbit, The Velveteen Rabbit,* and Henry Wadsworth Longfellow's *Paul Revere's Ride*, which was named 2004 Children's Book of the Year for Poetry by the Bank Street College Children's Book Committee. His illustrations for *The Wizard of Oz,* which is widely considered to be the quintessential illustrated version, were used as the scenic backdrops for a major television performance of the work. Charles Santore lives and works in Philadelphia.

The Classic Tale of Peter Rabbit Coloring Book
Illustrations copyright © 1986, 2017 by Charles Santore
Text copyright © 2017 by Appleseed Press Book Publishers LLC.

This is an officially licensed book by Cider Mill Press Book Publishers LLC.

Applesauce Press is an imprint of
Cider Mill Press Book Publishers
"Where Good Books Are Ready For Press"
PO Box 454
12 Spring Street
Kennebunkport, Maine 04046

VISIT US ON THE WEB!
www.cidermillpress.com

13-Digit ISBN: 9781604336863
10-Digit ISBN: 1604336862

Printed in The United States
1 2 3 4 5 6 7 8 9 0
First Edition